The Changer

EXPANDING CHILDREN'S HORIZONS

REBECCA HOUSE
PUBLISHING

The Changer

Tatiana Strelkoff

Rebecca House

Library of Congress Cataloging-in-Publication Data
Strelkoff, Tatiana, 1957-
p.   cm.
Summary: Woodman, an old Choctaw Indian, decides to teach ten-year old
Jeremy how to be a Changer, one who can become different kinds of animals.
ISBN 0-945522-03-7 : $ 12.95
1. Choctaw Indians–Juvenile fiction. [1. Choctaw Indians–Fiction.
2. Indians of North America– Fiction.   3. Human-animal
relationships–Fiction.]   I. Title.
PZ7.S91627Ch   1993
[Fic]–dc20   93-29477
                                                                      CIP
                                                                      AC

Rebecca House Publishing Company
1550 California Street, Suite 330
San Francisco, California 94109
[415] 752-1453

Printed in the United States of America.
ISBN 0-945522-03-7   SAN 247-1361
First Edition,   10 9 8 7 6 5 4 3 2 1

I dedicate this book to my sweetpeas,

Sasha and Pietro,
and my husband, Mimmo.

—Tatiana Strelkoff

ONLY ONE STAR FLICKERED dimly next to the crescent moon that night. Jeremy walked cautiously, unable to see the trees lining the country lane until he was right in front of them. Groping from one to the other, he reached out to feel the rough bark and pressed against it with relief. He paused before stepping forward to find the next tree. It was so dark, and Jeremy was frightened. He kept going because Woodman had told him that only on a night as black as this would he share his magic.

During the day, Jeremy ran and played among these same trees and ate their delicious apples. Now he couldn't even see them or the hard dirt road they grew beside. Only the familiar smell of apples was the same and it made him feel better. The old, weathered barn where he was heading was not far. During the day, when he stopped along the way to pick apples to eat later in the hay loft, it took him no time to get there. Tonight it seemed to take forever.

Why does it have to be such a black night for Woodman's magic to work? Jeremy wondered. He knew he was close now, but he still couldn't see the barn. He stopped and listened. There was no sound, no touch of wind, no rustling of leaves. Just stillness, and the smell of apples.

"Woodman?" Jeremy half whispered.

"I'm here, Jeremy," said a soft, kind voice.

Jeremy looked hard into the darkness. "I can't see you, Woodman. Where are you?"

"Just walk straight," said the voice. "I'm right here."

Jeremy took another step. Suddenly he could make out the form of a person; when he was right in front of him he could see Woodman's face.

The old man smiled and winked. "I've been waiting for you," he said, holding out his hands.

"It's so dark," said Jeremy. "I couldn't even see where I was going." He put his hands into Woodman's and felt his warm, rough skin. "Why does it have to be this dark before you show me anything?" he asked as they walked around to the back of the barn. He could feel the tall grass brushing against his pants.

"We can be stronger in the dark," said Woodman. "Sit here."

Jeremy sat down on an old crate next to the barn. "How are you going to show me anything if I can hardly see you?" he asked.

"You don't have to see me. Just listen."

Jeremy leaned back against the wall and looked at Woodman expectantly. He could see his body but could just barely make out his face.

Then he heard an owl call and, after that, the croak of a frog. Immediately after that a goat, a horse, a cat, and a chicken. But only Woodman was there, and he wasn't moving.

"Where did all those sounds come from?" Jeremy asked. "Did you make them, or were they real?"

Woodman did not answer right away. "They are all part of me," he then said quietly. "They are all me, and I am them."

Jeremy didn't understand what he meant. "Is this what you meant by magic?" asked Jeremy. "There's a man on TV that can do the same thing. He can even do them all at once."

"He imitates the animals. I am them."

"What do you mean?"

Woodman didn't answer. Instead, he lowered his hands to the ground, and Jeremy could vaguely see his dark brown skin becoming darker, and fur sprouting on the backs of his hands. His body began to shrink, smaller and smaller. His face grew long, his ears grew pointy, and a tail appeared. Jeremy stood up and stared hard. Woodman wasn't Woodman anymore. He was a fox!

"Oh, Woodman!" said Jeremy in a whisper. Part of him wanted to turn and race back home, and part of him couldn't move at all. "Woodman?"

The fox looked at him without moving, but when Jeremy reached out to touch its nose, he touched Woodman's hand instead. Jumping back, Jeremy let out a small cry.

"Woodman," he said loudly, trying to scare away his fear. "You were a fox!"

Woodman smiled. "You see, I can become one of the animals. I feel as they feel. I am hungry when they are hungry, cold when they are cold, in pain when they hurt."

"But how? How can you become an animal?" Jeremy held Woodman tightly by the hand to make sure that he stayed himself.

"From the days when my people lived free in the forest and shared nature's abundance with all the creatures made by God, there were those among us who could become the animals. It was a gift, a power that we passed from one generation to another. Sadly, I am the last Changer. Most of my people are dead, and those who remain have forgotten our ways. I am the last to believe. I want to give this gift to you."

Jeremy 's breath quickened at the thought. "You mean, teach me?"

"It's not just because of your Indian heritage. I've known and respected your mother all her life and, because of her, I know you. You feel nature in a way few people of your age do. You could be a Changer, if you can believe."

Jeremy was so astounded he didn't know what to say.

"Believing is the most important thing," Woodman continued in his soothing voice. "If you believe that you can change and believe it with your every breath, know it as you know your own name, then you can truly change. But if you have just one tiny doubt inside you, you will be unable to.

You will be like most other people, taking the earth we live on for granted."

"Like Jack at the post office?" Jeremy was thinking in disgust of all the animal heads hung up on the walls as trophies.

"Yes, like Jack at the post office and Redding at the garage and Doyle at the bank. None of them understands the feel of the earth, the touch of Mother Nature, her different smells and beautiful music. They have become foreigners in their own land, and they cannot be helped because they choose not to believe. Tell them that the wind plays music and they'll say you're a dreamer. Tell them that their horses long for freedom and they'll tell you that's why they want to break their spirit. Tell them that a coyote mourns his dead mate and they'll say you're crazy. They don't notice the motherly touch of a summer breeze or hear that insects sing their own particular songs. They think food is all their animals need, and there is no sadness in their hearts when they hunt. They believe they own the world and have the right to command and control it. They don't feel connected to this wonderful, magical, spiritual place that is our home."

In the silence that followed Woodman's words, Jeremy heard a distant owl.

"Do you really think that I could be a Changer like you?" asked Jeremy.

"Yes, if you believe you can."

"But how do you believe, Woodman?"

"That is what I'll teach you. We'll start tonight. You asked me why it had to be so black a night for me to show you. It's because in the daylight people see all the things that they have built—their clothes, cars, and houses. But at night, you

can't see in the ordinary way, so you have to feel. At night, you can begin to see differently, to see more deeply, the way Changers do. Are you ready?"

Jeremy nodded.

"All right. Close your eyes and imagine what it would feel like to be a horse running on your long, strong legs, your mane flying out behind you, the wind on your face and happiness in your heart. Feel it! Now, in this moment, you are the horse that longs for freedom."

"I can feel it!" said Jeremy, his legs tensing.

"Good! Good… Relax. Now, imagine you're a cat lying on the warm earth in the sun. The sun feels so warm and good on your shiny black fur, and you stretch first your front legs and then your back legs in pleasure and contentment."

Almost involuntarily, Jeremy stretched his arms down along his hips.

"Now imagine you're a bullfrog in the creek, squatting in the cool mushy mud that frogs love so much, singing your frog music."

"That's harder," said Jeremy. "I don't like frogs much."

"You don't have to like them, just feel like one!"

Jeremy shut his eyes tighter and imagined being a bull-frog. Half-hidden in the mud so just his big eyes showed, and raucously singing along with his frog friends, he marveled at how soothing the mud felt on his skin, how cool and inviting. For an instant he was thankful for the mud and the water and the sweet green grasses growing on the banks of the creek.

"You felt like a frog just then, didn't you?" asked Woodman.

"I did," said Jeremy in wonder.

"You see? This is how it starts. First you imagine and feel, then you slowly begin to believe that you can be, and then you change."

"Will it take a long time?"

"That depends on you. It depends on how strongly you believe."

Woodman and Jeremy continued imagining together for almost an hour, feeling what it's like to be a cow, a dog, a deer—even a turkey. For a second Jeremy had the impression that his neck had become long and skinny but when he touched it, it was the same as always.

Then Woodman said it was time to go home. As they walked back along the dirt road, Jeremy asked, "Do you hunt?"

"Animals hunt to survive," replied Woodman. "They do not kill randomly. And the entire animal is always eaten,

for what the coyote can't finish the fox will eat, and what the fox leaves the birds nibble on. Various insects and bacteria eat the remainder, so all that's left are the bones, which slowly decompose to feed and fertilize the earth. When my people hunt for food, they always speak to the spirit of the hunted animals, apologizing for taking their lives. We use the whole animal. Hunting is part of the natural order of things, a part of our survival, it should never be for our entertainment."

Woodman stopped when they were near Jeremy's house. "You can go on alone," he said, "you're almost home."

"When will you teach me more?" asked Jeremy, stopping too.

"You're learning fast, Jeremy, and I think you no longer need the darkness of night to feel the animals. We can meet tomorrow by the river, when the afternoon sun is low in the sky."

"Okay, tomorrow," said Jeremy, and he watched Woodman turn and walk away. He felt changed already, and as he climbed the oak tree into his bedroom window he suddenly pictured Jason's dog, left sitting for hours in the heat of the car while Jason played football with his friends. They wouldn't let Jeremy play, at ten he was still too young, and no one paid any attention to him when he told them Jason's dog seemed to be suffocating. He thought about his spotted cat, Buttons, how protective and loving she was with her kittens, cleaning them and feeding them and keeping their games close to her. Everything seemed so clear; it was as though the feelings of these animals were now his own. He shook his head in wonder as he lay in bed, thinking that Woodman was truly a remarkable old Indian. He wanted to become a Changer just like him. It was a wonderful gift, and he was honored and proud to have been the one chosen to carry it on.

JEREMY PLAYED OUTSIDE THE next day waiting
for the sun to sink low in the sky. He sat for a long time on
the fence watching the horses. They looked at him as
though they wanted to speak. Jeremy hoped that he would
soon learn to be them, to run and play with them and know
all the things that horses know. He lay on his back in the
field as well, watching the hawks glide on the wind, looping

gracefully and lazily up and down without ever moving their wings. He wanted to be up in the sky, too. He wanted to float high above the farms, fly free through the sky, dive down, then pull up, higher and higher toward the sun. In their part of Oklahoma the small farms and woodlands stretched all the way to the horizon, prairie grass and shady glens alternating along the long, flat vista. He could hear the cries of the hawks, and he knew they were telling him of all the places they had been and the marvels they had seen. His heart beat with excitement. He hoped it wouldn't take him long to learn how to become a Changer.

His thoughts were broken by the sound of a bell. He scanned the sky once more before running back home.

His mother had set the big wooden table in the yard, as she often did during the summer. His father and two older brothers were already sitting at their places.

"Go wash up, Jeremy," said his mother, brushing grass out of his hair as he ran by her.

Jeremy washed quickly and then sat down in his place between Joshua, who was thirteen, and John, who was fifteen. The table was loaded with sweet corn on the cob, fresh peas with baby onions, home-baked bread, and barbequed chicken. The family talked about the weather and the various things that needed to be done on the farm. Jeremy had done his chores that morning, all in a big rush so that he could meet Woodman in the afternoon. For once he didn't get one of his father's lectures about hard work and responsibility.

Just as Jeremy was scooping up the last of his fresh peaches with cream, his father said, "I have to go for supplies this afternoon and since Joshua and John have things to do, I want you to help me, Jeremy."

Jeremy looked at his father in dismay. "I can't, Dad," he said, not knowing what else to say exactly. "I have something important to do this afternoon!"

"What could you have to do that's so important? You're only ten!"

Jeremy wanted to keep the meeting with Woodman a secret, but he couldn't think of anything else to say.

"I have to meet Woodman," he said finally.

"Woodman? The old Indian? What in the world for?"

Everyone was staring at him. Jeremy could feel his face getting red. He hated that.

"Answer your father, Jeremy," said his mother, putting her hand on his arm gently.

"I just have to," Jeremy started, squirming in his chair. "He has to show me something important." He felt so uncomfortable under his father's stern gaze that tears came to his eyes.

His father's voice rose impatiently. "What could he possibly have to show you that's so important?"

"Special things," Jeremy blurted out. "Like how to change into an animal."

His brothers started snickering.

"Quiet," his father said. "Jeremy, that is nonsense. I don't want to hear any more silliness. Your responsibility is to help out on the farm, and I don't want you to talk to Woodman if he fills your head with such ridiculous stuff. I need your help today, and that's that."

"But I promised, Dad," Jeremy pleaded. "He'll be waiting for me. I've just got to go."

"That's enough, Jeremy!"

"Thomas," Jeremy's mother interjected quietly. "Let him be. He's still a child. He deserves some time for child's play."

"He's got to grow up sometime, and indulging him in Woodman's nonsense won't help."

"Hush," said Jeremy's mother sweetly. "I'll ask Binder to go with you. We hired him to help, didn't we? Let Jeremy be today. He's already done all his chores." She looked at Jeremy and smiled.

"You'll ruin this boy," muttered Jeremy's father. He ate the last of his peaches quickly, in an angry silence, and got up from the table. "You two get started," he said to John and Joshua. "I'll go get Binder." Glancing at his wife, he shook his head and walked off toward the tractor shed.

"It's not nonsense, Mom," said Jeremy, after his brothers had left. "It's not child's play either. Woodman really can change into an animal. I saw him. And he says he can teach me how, too."

"Yes, sweetheart," said his mother, getting up and kissing his cheek. "Go on and play, but don't be late for dinner."

Jeremy wanted to stay to convince her but was anxious to leave before his father came out with Binder. Besides, his mother was already humming a tune to herself, the way she always did when she was pleased.

It was still early, but Jeremy decided to wait by the river until Woodman came. He trotted off, practicing being a horse all the way to the river. Lying in the long grass on the bank, he imagined being all the animals that lived there, frogs and fish, squirrels and rabbits. He was wondering what it would be like to have rabbit ears when he heard someone call him. It was Woodman.

"I'm here," yelled Jeremy, scrambling to his feet.

Woodman came toward him, and although he was smiling Jeremy noticed that he was limping and in pain.

"Are you okay?" asked Jeremy.

"Yes, yes," said Woodman, waving his hand to say it was nothing. "Just the arthritis acting up, the old bones creaking." Lowering himself carefully, he breathed a sigh of relief and settled down on the ground. "It will soon be time for this old body..." he sighed. He leaned against the trunk of an oak tree and said, "Then the spirit will fly and join the hawk on the wind."

"Oh, no," said Jeremy, sitting down next to him. "There are all kinds of good medicines for arthritis, and besides, we have to be Changers together. It could never be the same without you."

"Not even a Changer lives forever, Jeremy, but he does have a special passage to the next world. You know, our people have a story...

> "The Wise One, who created the Earth and man and all the plants and animals, bestowed the gift of changing so that people and animals would always understand each other. The first Changer went out for the first time alone to the banks of the emerald-green river. He changed into a bear because two baby bear cubs were lost and crying for their mother, and he wanted to cross the river to reach them.
>
> "First Changer knew that the water was swift, and he knew that his body was heavy, but he was sure he could get across on the rocks, which were flat and mossy and many.
>
> "He stretched out his claws and widened his paws and stepped into the icy cold water, which gurgled and bubbled all around him in a tumbling white foam.
>
> "First Changer should have been looking down and watching every step he was taking, but he raised his eyes and called to the cubs who were watching and waiting, 'I'm coming!'

"Just then he slipped. Down and away in the frothy waters First Changer dove. Over and under, rolling and gasping, First Changer thought he was drowning, but he suddenly heard, from the gray rocky banks, the shouts of a band of beavers.

'Hang on, grab hold of this huge tree trunk,' they called. 'Grab it as it falls!' And just as First Changer came sweeping by them, the tree they had gnawed went down crashing.

"First Changer grabbed it as he was passing under, dug his claws in deep, and with the beavers urging him on, he scrambled to the bank and the slippery shore.

"He lay on his back there, panting and dripping, as the beavers all crossed the river. When they reached him he thanked them, then looked up and said loud and clear to the Wise One:

'You gave me a special gift, and the name First Changer, but today let me be known always as Brown Beaver.'

"And God agreed.

"When First Changer died, the Wise One let his spirit live as a beaver until it was time to go on to the next world. He knew it was what First Changer wanted. Ever since then, each Changer has chosen a second name to honor a special animal. When I die I will be the hawk, because my name is Black Hawk."

"Why did you choose that name?" asked Jeremy.

Woodman was quiet for a moment, and the light in his eyes paled. "I was married once, to the gentlest, most beautiful woman in Oklahoma. One day she went to gather berries after a rainstorm that had lasted days and days. The river had become wild, and she probably should not have

wandered out so soon after the rains. I knew before much time had passed that something was wrong. I set out to find her, but she could have gone anywhere, in any direction. I'd never seen the river so fierce, so angry and deafening. Hours passed. I walked and called, called and walked, fighting the thoughts that told me I had lost her. Suddenly I heard a hawk cry. He had seen her and came to find me, to tell me she had fallen in the river. I followed him to where she was, hanging onto a tree limb and almost unconscious. I was able to save her, and that was more important than my own life."

Woodman stopped speaking and stared ahead. Jeremy wanted to ask him more, but felt funny about breaking the silence. Finally, he couldn't help himself.

"Will I get a second name, too, when I become a Changer?" Jeremy asked.

"Of course," Woodman answered. "You never know which animal will come to you when you need help the most, but one always does."

"Any one would be perfect. I want all of them to be my friends."

Woodman smiled. "Let's begin your lessons then," he said, patting Jeremy gently on the head.

They sat on the bank by the river the rest of the afternoon as the sun dipped lower and lower in the sky and

finally descended below the horizon. They were so busy croaking and chirping, warbling and snorting, meowing and barking that they didn't realize that the air had grown cooler and that it was getting late. Jeremy felt so close to Woodman that his heart held a joy he had never known before.

Jeremy believed. He felt his skin go rough and bumpy like a frog's, and although he didn't look at Woodman he knew he was squatting like a frog beside him. He felt his fingers turn to feathers, and when he sang his breast swelled with pride. He sang more beautifully than any other wood thrush at the river that afternoon. He twitched his rabbit ears and heard sounds he had never heard before, the grasses whispering and the water seeping under ground. Each time he changed, his heart filled with love and appreciation for the animals he was beginning to know. He wanted to rub noses, touch wings, or cuddle together with paws, tails, and heads intertwined. Once he spread his hawk wings and trembled, arching his body to rise on the wind—when a strong hand tightly grasped his arm.

Jeremy opened his eyes to see Woodman standing beside him.

"Woodman, why did you stop me? I was ready to fly. I was a hawk!"

"You were, Jeremy. You were, and I'm proud of you. You are learning to be a real Changer, and before much time passes you will fly on the wind. But it's still too early. You're not ready. Be patient. We will fly together, but I must decide when the time is right."

Woodman let go of Jeremy's arm, and Jeremy looked around, realizing for the first time that it was late.

"I have to go, Woodman," he said. "I don't want Dad to get any angrier at me. Can we meet here tomorrow? I want to become a Changer."

"You will," said Woodman as they began the walk home along the river. "But being a Changer is not just about learning all the things the animals know. It's about helping them, being a part of their lives and a brother to all your different animal siblings. You must be able and wise. Be patient now, my young friend."

"I'll do everything just the way you say, Woodman. I promise."

"The river will be our meeting place," said Woodman as they parted at the wooden bridge. "We will meet tomorrow at the same time as today."

"What if I can't come? What if they won't let me? How will you know not to wait for me?"

"I'll know. Birds are such gossips!" Woodman winked and headed off across the bridge.

How different everything seemed to Jeremy! The weeds and wild grasses smelled fresh and sweet. The expanse of meadow on either side of the road made his heart feel just as open and vast. He spread his arms wide and looked up into the twilight blue-and-tangerine sky. The fragrant breeze brought him special thoughts. He was so much a part of everything—the earth, the sky, and the wind—that he felt new inside.

"I don't ever want to lose this feeling," he said aloud, turning in a circle to address everything living and moving around him. "I want to stay this way forever!"

JEREMY MET WOODMAN MANY times in the weeks that followed. Somehow, Woodman always knew when Jeremy could come and would wait for him on those days. The weather slowly changed before them, and every week the air cooled and the animals they saw were busier and less playful. Jeremy no longer told his father where he went, but his brothers knew, and they always teased him as he was leaving for his lesson.

"Only babies play make-believe at your age," said Joshua, "or girls!"

"Yeah, little girls!" John echoed.

"It's not make-believe! You don't know anything about it!"

"I wasn't doing stuff like that when I was ten. I was playing football or out fishing." Joshua threw a make-believe football in a long pass to John.

"You've got to grow up, Jeremy," John said, catching the invisible football. "Aren't you interested in important things, like getting on the football team—or girls?"

"This is important! I'll be able to help the animals—and even learn to fly." Jeremy's good sense told him he should just ignore them, but he couldn't help himself.

"That crazy old Indian is filling your head with garbage. He'll be dead soon anyway!" John taunted.

That made Jeremy furious. But when he told Woodman what they said, Woodman just smiled.

"Never let them bother you, Jeremy. Just let their words go by without touching you. I don't need them to believe me and you don't either."

"I'll show them. I'll show them right in front of them. Then they'll be amazed and wish they could do it, too."

Woodman shook his head. "No one needs to know. You don't have to show anybody anything. If people knew, everything would be different. You'd become a television celebrity, a boy wonder. Instead of helping the animals you'd end up traveling the world for scientific experiments. Changing should be your way to help, to give something extra of yourself. You don't need to boast about what you do, you just do it."

Jeremy didn't say anything else because Woodman led him down the bank to the river to show him where the beavers were building their lodges, but he repeated to himself, "They'll see. They'll be sorry!"

The anger passed because he was so busy he forgot about it. Little by little he was becoming a Changer. He began to understand the squirrels chattering in the trees. Rabbits came and let him touch them, and one mother deer even let him kiss her fawn on the nose.

Many times Jeremy longed to follow his new friends, swim with the beavers down the river or scamper with the rabbits into the thickets of the woods, but Woodman always kept him at their spot by the river.

One day, walking home, Jeremy was unusually quiet.

"What is it, Jeremy?" asked Woodman, stopping to study his face.

"School starts soon, Woodman, and I won't be able to go out until I finish my homework and it'll already be dark then."

"We'll have the weekends, and holidays."

"I have chores on Saturday and church on Sunday and Dad will never let me go if I tell him what I'm doing. Why won't you let me change now, while there's still time? Why can't we go walking with the deer, or fly? I'm ready now. I'm a Changer."

"You've learned very fast, Jeremy. I knew when I chose you that you could become a Changer, and you haven't disappointed me. But one day you will have to change into an animal by yourself. It's dangerous sometimes, and you won't have me beside you, so you must learn everything there is to know.

"Fall is coming, with winter fast behind. Life is hard when the snows come and ice hangs from the trees and hardens the river. Remember, becoming an animal isn't a game, Jeremy. You have the gift for a purpose. You must use it wisely. You know, when you take a second name it's because some animal has given itself to help you. After that, you make a commitment, and you can never go back."

Jeremy didn't say anything else, but Woodman seemed to know what he was thinking, and before they parted he held him by the shoulders and looked into his eyes.

"I must be sure that you will be able to be a Changer when I am gone. It's easy now, we both believe together, but it's harder when you must believe alone. Be patient, Jeremy, the time will come."

Jeremy nodded and turned toward home. Though the sun was still warm and the sky was still blue, the air these days smelled of drying leaves and burning wood, and Jeremy could hear the busy preparation of the animals. "Winter will be very cold and not long in coming," he heard them say.

Jeremy thought about Woodman. Did Woodman really need to be with him? Jeremy was sure he could change alone. He didn't want to be treated like a baby. There was so much he could do as a Changer. He'd show his brothers first, so that they'd stand there with their mouths open. He wouldn't teach them how either. He'd show his parents, too, to prove that Woodman wasn't crazy.

And he'd show Woodman, too. Woodman was old, but strong as ever. It was just that his arthritis acted up once in a while. They would have plenty of time together for

Woodman to teach him what he still had to know. But he would show Woodman that he didn't need his protection. He could change by himself, anywhere he wanted to.

Jeremy stood for a moment at the gate in front of his house. The sun was setting early now, at five thirty. It was not cold, but clouds were piled up along the horizon. "Tonight," thought Jeremy as he opened the gate and walked into the yard. "I'll sneak out tonight and change by myself."

IN BED THAT NIGHT Jeremy lay with his eyes wide open, waiting to hear his parents walk up the creaky wooden stairs and shut their bedroom door. He could see the sky through the open curtains of his window. The moon was full, and the clouds had begun to spread out across the sky. It wasn't windy, but Jeremy could feel a breeze that carried a hint of fall.

He waited for a long while to be sure that his parents were asleep. Then he got up slowly and quietly put on his tennis shoes. Crawling out of his window onto the huge oak branch, he climbed down the tree to the ground. The moon was so bright that even when clouds passed over it Jeremy could see. He crept through the yard and, instead of opening the squeaky gate, climbed over it. He was heading toward the old barn where he had first learned about being a Changer. He thought it would be the best place. He was so anxious, so excited, that he didn't notice that the clouds had stopped moving and were hanging heavy in the sky.

He was running fast now. "A fox," he said as he reached the barn and went around to the back. "Like the first time."

His heart beat rapidly as he stood still in the grass. He lowered his head and closed his eyes. Dropping slowly to the ground, he twitched his ears and blinked.

There was something in the air. He couldn't see ahead, only to the sides, and he turned his head, sniffing. The ground was wet under his paws and the longer blades tickled his nose. He was ready.

From behind the barn he crept slowly into the field. He brushed his tail against a tree to feel that he really had a tail.

The small red fox trotted briskly through the field, pausing sometimes to sniff the air and the earth. He held his head high and pranced like a show pony at the circus. The air was cool, and though the moon was now barely able to filter through the thick clouds, the fox saw everything that moved. Field mice scattered in all directions at the sound of his approach, and squirrels scuttled up the trees. The fox moved with a steady pace through the damp field.

The breeze picked up, and the fox knew that rain was coming soon. There was also something else in the wind, and without changing his gait the red fox changed direction.

A cluster of farm buildings stood on the edge of the field. In a small enclosure penned with wire were several dozen hens and roosters sitting on their perches.

The first wind-blown raindrops stung the fox's eyes as he slowed his gait. By the time he began his stealthy approach toward the southern side of the pen, the rain was falling thickly onto his damp fur. The dirt around the fence was quickly turning to mud, and the bottom of the wire was already becoming visible as the fox neared the chicken coop.

Belly to the ground, the fox crept forward, its eyes half shut to the rain and its breath shallow and soft.

Suddenly, many dogs started barking wildly. Whirling, the fox leaped back toward the field just as a window was thrown open and a light switched on, illuminating his red coat as he streaked across the yard back toward the fallow ground.

The fox ran faster through the stinging, cold rain, the dogs on his trail. Leaping the last few feet to the field, he heard a whistling zip by close to his ear. More shots were almost drowned out in the clamorous barking. Already, the dogs were right behind, and the fox ran blindly, as fast as he could go.

Then, just to his right, another dog appeared, and in startled terror the fox veered to the left. The dog was barking but the fox only heard the blood pounding in his ears. Already he knew it was hopeless. He could smell the dog's scent, and as he stopped and turned to fight in desperation, he was hit by a dark form hurtling through the air for his throat.

The fox fell hard as the dog seized him.

"You're Jeremy!"

Jeremy opened his eyes. He was lying in the rain and Woodman was on top of him, panting heavily and holding his arm in a grip that was making it go numb. Jeremy was also panting, and surprised to find that he was crying too. He could feel his heart aching, and though he couldn't remember why, he was more frightened than he'd ever been. He could hear dogs barking and men's voices through the rain. Pushing Woodman slightly, he rolled over in the wet grass and stood up.

Woodman was still sitting on the ground and struggling to catch his breath. Two men appeared behind the dogs, who were running in excited circles sniffing the wet air and whining like confused, frightened pups. Jeremy recognized Joe Tanner and his eldest son.

"Who's out this time of night in this weather?" yelled Joe. The dogs milled around his feet. "What's with these dogs?" he growled to his son, kicking one of the animals away.

"Jeremy!" said Joe as he walked closer, lowering his shotgun to the ground. "What are you doing here? What happened?" He looked at Woodman, who was standing shakily, leaning on Jeremy for support. "I was after a fox trying to kill my chickens," said Joe. "I saw it when I shot, I'm sure. Now it's gone and instead I find you two!"

Jeremy knew he had to explain, but he stood dumbly as the rain ran down his face, his shoes soaked through to his socks.

The dogs were still whining, their tails between their legs.

"What's going on?" yelled Joe.

"Well, we ran into a bit of trouble," said Woodman, letting go of Jeremy. "Jeremy and I were going home but the

rain surprised us and somehow we got confused and ended up here. Your dogs scared us and we fell when we started running in the mud."

"Going home at this hour?" asked Joe. "Shut up!" he yelled at the dogs, threatening them with his boot. "I could've killed you," he added, looking at Woodman angrily.

"Jeremy just wanted to have some fun before school started," said Woodman reassuringly. "He really shouldn't be out this late just to do some frog-gigging. His father would be angry if he knew, but a boy needs to do what we all did, once in a while. You won't get him in trouble, will you?"

"Out in the rain frog-gigging?" Joe shook his head. "I'm soaked to the bone, we lost the fox, and you're telling me about frogs. Get on home, Jeremy. I won't say nothin' to your dad, but get home now."

Jeremy nodded, Woodman took him by the arm, and they began walking back across the field.

Joe Tanner stood for a minute watching them walk away, then threw his shotgun to his son and stomped off toward the house cussing the rain and foxes and crazy Indians.

Woodman walked Jeremy to the old barn and sat him down on an empty crate inside. Jeremy hadn't said a word. Now, as Woodman looked at him sternly, he started to shiver.

"Why did you go out on your own, Jeremy? You weren't ready. I warned you."

Jeremy looked up into Woodman's brown, wrinkled face and felt tears in his eyes. "I don't remember."

"You changed into a fox, Jeremy, but you weren't ready. You became a fox, but not completely, so you didn't do what a fox does. You couldn't change back, either, because you lost yourself when you changed, you couldn't remember

being you. A fox wouldn't have run to an open field where it tires faster than a dog. It would have tricked the dogs by hiding downwind, tracking back and confusing them. A Changer is able to be both the fox and himself. He can do as the fox does, but he knows that he is not the fox. Right now, you are only able to be one or the other, and if you don't learn all there is to know you will not do either well."

"I wanted to change on my own," said Jeremy. "I thought I could." He was shivering so much his head hurt.

Woodman sat down next to him and hugged him. "Youth has always been impatient," he said. They sat together in silence, Woodman's arm around Jeremy. At last, when Jeremy's shaking subsided, Woodman pulled him up and directed him out of the barn and toward his house. "It is the nature of people to strike out before they are ready. But sometimes one learns, as you did tonight, that the counsel of the aged is sound. I have been a Changer since my grandfather took me out at the age of ten to the wild forest where the town of Jennings stands today. For two years we went to the same small glen before we went any place else, and it wasn't until I had become a man that he allowed me to go alone. I was like you, sure that I was ready, but I would have never disobeyed Gray Wolf."

"I'm sorry, Woodman. I know I shouldn't have," said Jeremy. "I won't again, I promise."

"I know. As it is, we do not have much time. My days are ending, and you will have to be able long before I was. How quickly the time goes now, each year shorter than the last. And I still need to show you that it's not just for the joy of being the animals that we become Changers, but to help them, to use this gift to help in a way no one else can..." Woodman trailed off, and they walked for a while in silence.

"I'd never go frog-gigging," said Jeremy, when they were almost home. "I think it's horrible to blind frogs with a flashlight and then stab them to death. And I don't like frogs' legs anyway."

"I know you wouldn't. I wouldn't have chosen you to be a Changer if you did. But I had to say something Tanner would believe."

"I'd never kill anything," said Jeremy, tears in his eyes again.

When they got to Jeremy's house, Woodman boosted Jeremy over the fence.

"Dry off and get warm quickly," he called softly as Jeremy walked toward the oak outside his window. "I'll be waiting for you tomorrow."

SUMMERTIME WAS ENDING and small changes took place day by day, changes Jeremy had never noted so vividly. The leaves of the trees went from deep green to burnished hues of gold and red and yellow. Morning was later in coming, while night advanced more quickly, leaving fewer daylight hours. Though it was still sunny the sun gave less heat, barely able to penetrate Jeremy's sweater.

The animals knew preparations had to be made for winter and they had little time to do it. The beavers worked along the banks of the river where Jeremy and Woodmen met, as did the squirrels and rabbits. The fawns had grown into strong, young deer. Every day the sky was dotted by birds in flight, leaving for their winter homes.

Jeremy no longer needed to close his eyes to become an animal. His desire was all that was necessary. He was amazed at how fast he was learning. The beavers showed him how they built their lodges with mud that would freeze in the winter and make their homes safe and warm. They told him how they saved twigs and small branches in the mud at the bottom of the river so that they could eat them during the long, bleak winter. The squirrels showed him how nuts could be stowed away under the yellow leaves. The deer explained how they could find green shoots and leaves to eat even when they were hidden by the snow.

"Hardships are caused by the weather," the fox said, "but my worst enemy is people who do not respect nature."

When Jeremy came home each evening he was quiet and thoughtful. His mother worried that he might be sick. Jeremy was still her baby, her last child, and she fretted about him more than her other sons. They were older and she could no longer influence them, but she knew Jeremy was going to be special. He liked to read and sing and spend time with her in the kitchen just talking.

Jeremy felt his mother didn't believe him, but he told her about the changing anyway. She was the only person he could tell. Sometimes she even agreed that a group of beavers was like a family and that foxes should just be left alone, even though they did kill chickens sometimes. Jeremy usually felt better after talking with his mother. She

reminded him that he wasn't the only one who cared about the animals.

School started at the end of September. Jeremy knew most of the children in his class, and all the teachers. He especially liked the librarian, who always found him interesting books to read.

Autumn was unusually cool that year. Jeremy had known that it was going to be a long, hard winter since August, because he heard the animals talking about it.

Weekends were now the times Woodman and Jeremy got together. Jeremy's mother cheerfully distracted his father with stories and chores and covered up for Jeremy when he was gone.

Woodman said, "Your mother is part Choctaw Indian and probably believes you, deep inside, even if she doesn't say so."

Jeremy didn't know what to think, but he appreciated his mother for her caring. He always brought her something when he came home, a wildflower or a polished stone or a feather. She would put what he brought in a wooden box, the same box that held all his baby teeth. It was her special box, and he was glad to know she kept his gifts there.

His mother was beautiful. She was blonde and had high, flat cheekbones like the Indian women Jeremy saw sometimes when his father took him to the rodeo. She was the one who told him that the name Oklahoma was made up of two Choctaw words put together meaning "people" and "red."

One Sunday afternoon Jeremy's mother made a pineapple upside-down cake. Jeremy's father loved pineapple upside-down cake and settled down with it at the table in the warm kitchen. He didn't even notice that Jeremy had changed clothes and put on his heavy sheepskin jacket and cap.

Jeremy's mother winked at him as he passed the open kitchen door. Without saying anything, Jeremy opened the front door and went quietly outside.

In just a few weeks the weather had transformed their entire farm. All the trees were bare, the ground hard and brittle. With the leaves gone from the trees the farm seemed small, and Jeremy could see far across the fields. The land was cold and gray. The wind was blowing masses of clouds across the sky. Jeremy thought it might snow. If it did, it would be the first time in history that snow had come so early. Being a Changer had taught him many things, and he was sure that it would snow that night if the temperature dropped low enough.

Shoving his hands into his pockets, he headed toward the river. The wind was powerful and it was hard to walk. By the time he got to the riverbank he felt tired and drained. The wind was getting stronger, whooshing through the branches of the trees and making his cheeks sting. Woodman wasn't there yet, so Jeremy just stood and listened to the sounds of the forest. All the animals he'd grown accustomed to seeing were gone, hidden in their homes.

The wind howled and wailed, and Jeremy shivered, pulling his cap down lower on his head and feeling strangely uneasy. Woodman had never been late before. Maybe something had happened.

Suddenly he heard a cawing, and looking up he saw a hawk circling above him, fighting the wind. Its form was a dark blot on the gray sky. It was calling him, and Jeremy knew what it was saying. A wolf was in trouble, caught in a trap down stream, and Woodman needed his help.

Jeremy started running along the bank. The wind was blowing at his back, pushing him with gusts of cold air. His boots were heavy and it was hard to run. His heart beat fast, both from the exertion and from fear. Something was wrong, and something worse was still to come. He could feel it.

Coming around a bend in the river he saw a terrified wolf struggling in the middle of the water, a beaver beside it. The beaver dove under the water and came up again for air. It was Woodman.

Just as Jeremy reached them, the first snowflakes started to fall. He threw off his coat and hat, stood motionless at the water's edge for an instant and looked hard at the struggling wolf. Then Jeremy changed.

It was a shiny beaver that dove into the water and swam easily to the wolf. Giving the water a hard slap with his tail, Jeremy dove under Woodman, who was already near the bottom, tugging at a tree trunk sunk in the mud. The wolf's bloody foot was caught in an iron trap, and the trap was snagged on a branch. It was useless to pull on the submerged trunk. It was probably a lot bigger than it seemed, half-buried as it was, and it was heavy.

The second beaver swam to where the trap was caught and began gnawing on the branch, trying to break it off from the rest of the tree. He surfaced several times for air and tried to calm the thrashing wolf who was churning up the water and making it harder to see. Finally he gnawed through the branch, and, with one last tug, the wolf pulled free and swam to shore with the trap and the branch still attached. The beavers swam to shore also and crawled out.

Jeremy dropped onto the bank, shook the water out of his hair, and looked around. Woodman was standing beside him, panting and dripping, and the wolf was whining and licking his mangled paw.

"Are you okay, Woodman?" asked Jeremy, getting up to go to him.

"It was good you came," panted Woodman. "I kept trying to pull the trunk out but wasn't strong enough, didn't think." His face was ashen and he couldn't stop shaking from the cold and exhaustion.

"Woodman, you're not all right," said Jeremy, taking his limp hand.

"The wolf—get his paw out of that," panted Woodman.

Snow was falling heavily, swirling around them, and Jeremy reached out with stiff fingers to unlock the trap. It was snapped tightly on the wolf's paw, and Jeremy could hardly see through the flying snow to pry it open. The wind whistled and crashed through the trees and a hawk was screeching above, flooding Jeremy's heart with panic. He couldn't get the trap open.

Desperately Jeremy searched his pockets for the knife he always carried. It was small, but solid and sturdy. Closing his numb fingers around it with relief, Jeremy pulled it out and

sawed off a short, fat chunk of the branch. He pried open the trap with the knife and wedged the branch in. The wolf still could not pull his paw out, but Jeremy was able to get his fingers into the trap and pull the jaws apart as hard as he could. The wolf was free!

Jeremy couldn't hear anything the wolf said as he sat next to him, licking his paw, because of the roaring wind and screeching hawk flying circles above him. He turned back to help Woodman but stopped short and caught his breath in horror. Woodman was sitting up against a tree, his face as white as the snow. His eyes were wide open, glassy and still. Woodman was dead.

Jeremy wanted to run to him but couldn't move. He wanted to scream but no sound came. He just stared at the gnarled hands lying peacefully in Woodman's lap as the hawk screeched and cried.

Finally, the words flew out of his mouth. "Woodman! Woodman!" He went to the tree and stood directly in front of Woodman, afraid to touch him. "Oh, no, Woodman!"

Jeremy twirled around quickly as though someone were behind him. "Woodman, I can't see! I can't get home!" he yelled, turning back to look at the old Indian. "Woodman, I can't get home!"

Kneeling in the snow, he put his hands on Woodman's shoulders and, unable to control himself, began shaking him.

"Woodman, help me get home!"

The wind carried away his words before he heard them. The snow was blinding, the wind freezing his ears, and all the while that hawk kept screeching horribly. Suddenly, Jeremy realized that the hawk was trying to get his attention. He looked up into the whirling whiteness and saw its

black body battling to keep its course. Through the wind, Jeremy listened to its words. Woodman's spirit was in the hawk–and would guide him home.

Jeremy stood up, his eyes riveted on the black dot in the turbulent white sky. For a second he glanced back down at Woodman, wondering if he should bury him, but the hawk's cries changed his mind. "There is no need, no time," the hawk said. Woodman's spirit was free from that body, and soon it would be too late for Jeremy. He had to get home now. Wet and cold, he could freeze to death as he was. The first thing he had to do was to change.

Just then the wounded wolf stood and rubbed against Jeremy's leg. "A wolf–change into a wolf," the wolf said. A wolf's fur would keep him warm, and though wounded, the wolf he had freed would help him travel home.

Jeremy looked down at the wolf and stared directly into his friendly gray eyes.

Two Gray Wolves Walked cautiously along the river, their heads down against the wind and their ears flattened. The blizzard raged around them. Sometimes they stopped so the wounded wolf could rest, but only for a few seconds. The snow would cover them completely if they lingered.

The wind was so fierce that they had to fight against it for every step. Their eyes were nearly closed because of the snow. Sometimes the younger wolf would falter, step into a snow-covered hole and almost fall, but the older wolf would rub against him to calm him and help him keep going. Finally they came to the spot where Woodman and Jeremy used to practice. Again the older wolf rubbed against the other, butting him gently with his head. Then he turned and limped away, disappearing quickly into the swirling white storm.

Jeremy looked around. The moment the older wolf had disappeared he had picked up the scent of people. Jeremy changed back to himself and tried to run in that direction but sank into snow with each step. In less than a minute he was panting and exhausted. He couldn't see his house, but he knew which way it was and struggled toward it. Through the snow, he could just make out someone else fighting to walk, coming in his direction. He saw a long, black coat whipping and flapping as though it were alive. It was his mother's coat! Jeremy screamed, "Here, Mother, I'm here!"

But he knew she couldn't hear him. She was stumbling from one tree to the next, hugging the trunks, and he realized that she, too, was shouting.

"Mother, I'm here," Jeremy screamed again, trying to run.

She turned then, and saw him, and shouted again. In that instant there was a horrible cracking, like a ripping in the sky. He saw a dead tree split under the force of the wind and begin to topple–right next to where his mother stood.

He could not get to her, could not reach her in time. In one brief instant he stretched out his body and arms and, as a wolf, leaped the distance and threw himself against her. She tumbled backward down a low slope covered with snow. Behind them the tree hit the ground with a deafening crash.

Jeremy's mother, frightened and amazed, struggled to free herself. The wolf was still on top of her, and in her effort to get up she did not realize that the wolf was hurt. Her coat seemed to bind her and she struggled to push the wolf away and stand. The wolf yelped in pain as she clambered to her knees, and she realized it was wounded. Just then she saw her husband and John come running from a distance.

She tried to stand, fighting to keep her balance in the snow. As she turned toward her husband, she saw him lower his rifle to aim at the wolf.

"Good God, Thomas, no!" she screamed, throwing herself in front of the wolf and stretching out her arms. "It's Jeremy!"

"Marilyn, get away! What's wrong with you?" yelled Jeremy's father.

She ran toward him. "Don't shoot! Don't shoot!"

"My God, Marilyn! John, get your mother."

Jeremy's brother tried to hold her, but she wrenched herself free, trying to grab the rifle out of her husband's hands. They fought in the freezing wind, and twice the rifle went off wildly into the sky. In the panic the wolf pulled himself to his feet and limped away for cover in the tangle of trees and branches and fallen snow.

Holding his wife and hugging her close, Jeremy's father threw the rifle to John and nodded in the direction of the wolf. John understood and went off after it.

THE GRAY WOLF WAS LIMPING slowly toward
the river. One foot was useless, so he hobbled on three, trying to get through the deepening snow. When John broke
through the thicket, he could see the wolf in the distance,
slowly making its way up the riverbank. Stopping, he lowered
the site on his rifle. The wolf sensed that John was behind
him, and as he turned to look, John squeezed the trigger. In

that instant a young deer shot out from behind a clump of trees and caught the bullet squarely in its chest. Without a sound it fell.

The wolf howled. John stared at the fallen deer in amazement. The wolf stared at John, and for a long moment neither one moved. Then the wolf climbed awkwardly up the bank and disappeared over the side.

Jeremy sat in the snow rubbing his ankle. He knew it was swelling because it was throbbing and his boot was tight. His heart ached with a sadness too great for tears, and though he could hear his brother coming up the riverbank he did not call to him.

"Jeremy! Are you okay?"

Jeremy turned slightly as his brother ran up to him.

"We've been searching for you everywhere. Where have you been?"

Jeremy looked down at his ankle without answering.

"Are you hurt?" John crouched down next to him and tried to look into his face. Jeremy could see the questions in his eyes. "Your ankle?"

Jeremy nodded.

"Can you walk?"

Jeremy nodded again.

"Mom and Dad have been really scared. Mom's gone totally hysterical. We've got to tell them you're okay."

John hauled Jeremy to his feet. "Here, let me help you," he said, putting one arm around Jeremy to support him.

They started back down the riverbank. It was still snowing, but the wind was beginning to weaken. When they came upon the body of the deer it was already almost totally buried in the snow. Jeremy said nothing but looked up at John.

"I didn't mean to kill it," said John, as though Jeremy had accused him. "I was aiming for a wolf. A wolf attacked Mom. I was about to shoot it, but this deer just ran in front of me. Could've had rabies, that wolf! Should've shot it, but it got away, even though it was limping…" John's voice trailed off and he looked at Jeremy, but Jeremy didn't say a word. He kept his eyes on the ground and continued walking. He didn't look up again until he heard his mother call him.

"Jeremy! Oh, Jeremy!" Jeremy's mother broke away from her husband and ran to her son. She hugged him fiercely, tears running down into his hair. She held his face for a moment and looked into his eyes, then she pressed him to her again and turned to John.

"Is he all right?"

"He's hurt his ankle. It's probably sprained, but he can walk."

Looking both confused and relieved, Jeremy's father encircled his wife and Jeremy with his arms and hugged them briefly. "Let's get him home," he said to his wife. "It's freezing."

Still holding him close, Jeremy's mother began walking home. John tried to help, but Jeremy pulled away and pressed closer to his mother. John stopped and watched them walk away together, Jeremy reaching around his mother's waist as she held him tightly around the shoulders. He glanced at his father, then followed them without a word.

It took a while to warm up, even with the hot water bottle at his feet and two quilts on the bed. He drank two cups of tea, which he hated, to stop shivering. Jeremy's mother was sitting silently on the side of the bed, holding his hand and looking out the bedroom window.

"Got through to Dr. Johnson," said Jeremy's father, coming into the bedroom. John followed and stood in the doorway. "The wind's died down, so he'll be able to come soon. Said he's never seen such a freak storm in all the time he's lived here. How's my boy?" he added, looking at Jeremy. There was so much love in his eyes Jeremy could feel it all the way across the room.

"Okay, Dad. I'm okay."

"Good. Everything's going to be fine. You see, Marilyn, everything's just fine."

Jeremy's mother looked at him and smiled, but she didn't say anything.

"Just fine," Jeremy's father repeated.

There was an odd silence in the room, and Jeremy closed his eyes to escape it.

"You were out with Woodman, weren't you?" asked his father patiently.

Jeremy opened his eyes. "Yes, but we got separated when it started snowing, and I got lost."

"Wasn't much help to you, was he?"

Jeremy looked at him but didn't say anything. He didn't mean to be unkind, Jeremy knew that. He would never understand. It would be no use to explain. "It doesn't matter. Woodman is dead," said Jeremy sadly.

His father stared at him. He seemed not to know how to respond, then blurted, "Well, thank God you're safe." He shook his head. "Freak storm anyhow. Who'd have known?" He smiled, but Jeremy could see his jaw muscles tightening.

"Why don't you two go downstairs and make us some sandwiches?" said Jeremy's mother. "I think we could all use some food."

Jeremy's father and brother hesitated for a moment and then left. Jeremy's mother tightened her hand around Jeremy's and gazed again out the window. Snow was still falling, but much lighter, and the sky seemed to be clearing.

"How did Woodman die?" asked his mother gently.

Jeremy looked at her, but she did not look away from the window.

"His heart, I think," Jeremy said.

His mother nodded, and Jeremy waited for her to ask him something else.

"Did you get a second name today, along with Changer?" she asked. She took him into her arms as he answered.

"Leaping Deer," he said. The sadness was still in his heart, but a sense of pride and purpose began to fill him as he looked into his mother's eyes. Strongest of all, he felt a powerful love for Woodman and for the deer that had given him his new name. Because of them, he was now a real Changer.

COLOPHON

Text illustrations were drawn in pencil
on Strathmore 500 Bristol Paper.
Cover illustration was done in watercolor and Prismacolor
on Strathmore 500 Bristol Paper.

Body type is 14 point Adobe Weiss
set on 17 points of lead.

Other than original illustrations, all production was
performed electronically.

Text printed on 70 pound Finch Opaque.